THE STAFF

THE STAFF

by MIKE THALER

pictures by JOSEPH SCHINDELMAN

Alfred A. Knopf   New York

For Naomi

THE STAFF

Once upon a time there was an old gypsy who had two sons, Eema and Tuma. One day when they were crossing a great forest he stopped and leaned against a large rock.

"This is my last journey," he said. "But as it is an end for me it is a beginning for you. All I have to leave you is my staff. Each take half and use it as you will."

Tuma took the staff and Eema held his
father's hand as it grew cold.

Then they divided the staff,
and the two boys went on
through the forest alone.

When it grew dark they stopped and built
a fire. "What are you going to make of your
half?" asked Eema.

"I am going to make a blowgun to hunt for
food and to protect us," said Tuma. "What are you
going to make?"

"A flute," said Eema.

"A flute!" said Tuma.

"A flute," said Eema.

The next morning Tuma made a
blowgun and went out hunting.
Eema stayed in camp and
made his flute.

The day passed. In the evening Tuma
returned tired and angry, for all day he had not
been able to catch a single animal or bird.

Much to his surprise he found Eema surrounded
by all the animals and birds of the forest. The
wild hens laid eggs for them, and the squirrels
and chipmunks brought nuts and berries. When
they had eaten, the two boys went to sleep. And
the animals and birds returned to their nests
and burrows in the forest.

In the middle of the night the boys were wakened by a thunderous crashing.

"Don't be scared. I'll protect you," said Tuma, grabbing his blowgun.

With a final mighty crash
and a fall of branches,
a giant stood before them.

"What are you doing in my
forest?" He shouted
so loudly that all the leaves
fell off the trees
and covered the two boys.

Eema poked his head out of the leaves.

"We've come to play music for you," he said, holding up his flute. He began to play the happiest song he knew. Then he played the saddest song he knew. A big tear rolled down the giant's cheek and splashed on Tuma.

"Now what can I do for you?" asked the giant, drying his eyes.

"We are trying to reach the edge of the forest," said Eema.

The giant put the two boys on his shoulders and carried them over the trees and out of the forest.

"This is as far as I dare go," said the giant when they had reached the edge, "for there is a king and his army of which I am very afraid. They will surely shoot arrows at me, and that is why I stay in the forest."

Eema and Tuma waved goodbye as the giant went back in the forest. Then they started down the road that stretched in front of them.

They traveled all morning till about noontime,
then suddenly the road began to shake.

A gold carriage with a beautiful princess passed
by, almost running over them.

"She was beautiful," said Tuma.

"Let us go that way," said Eema,
pointing down the road.

By evening they came to a great castle surrounded by a moat.

"How will we get in?" said Tuma.

But Eema had already started to play his flute, and the music floated over the moat, in through the castle window, and into the princess's ear.

She ordered the drawbridge lowered, and soon the boys were being led into the castle.

They were brought before the king where Eema
played, and immediately was appointed the
court musician. As for Tuma, he made a request
to join the army and learn to be a great warrior.

So the boys grew up as did the princess who became more beautiful every day.

Then one day the king who spent all his time worrying about the giant read a proclamation:

"Whosoever shall bring me the head of the forest giant shall marry the princess."

Tuma, who was now a brave warrior, vowed that he would be the one.

Eema said that he would like to try, in his own way, as he loved the princess dearly.

So the two rode out—Tuma in gold armor on a white horse.

And Eema on a donkey he had
borrowed from the castle cook.

They were gone for two days and two nights.
Everyone waited and wondered. On the third day
the earth around the castle shook.

"It's the giant," shouted the king.

"He must have killed Eema," cried the princess.

"And now he'll kill us," cried the king,
hiding behind the throne.

Then suddenly, the princess saw Eema
riding on the giant's shoulder.

"Don't be afraid," he shouted. "I know the
king only wanted the giant's head, but I thought
he would enjoy much more the whole giant."

Now everyone could see there was nothing to
fear, and a cheer went up for Eema and the giant.

Not long thereafter, Eema and the princess were married. The king and the giant became good friends and played chess together every day.

And when Tuma returned to the castle, he decided it was time to learn the flute.

Text set in Cloister, on the Linotype
Composed by Howard O. Bullard, Inc., New York, New York
Printed by Reehl Litho., Inc., Milbrook, New York
Bound by A. Horowitz & Son, Bookbinders, Clifton, New Jersey
Typography by Thomas Morley